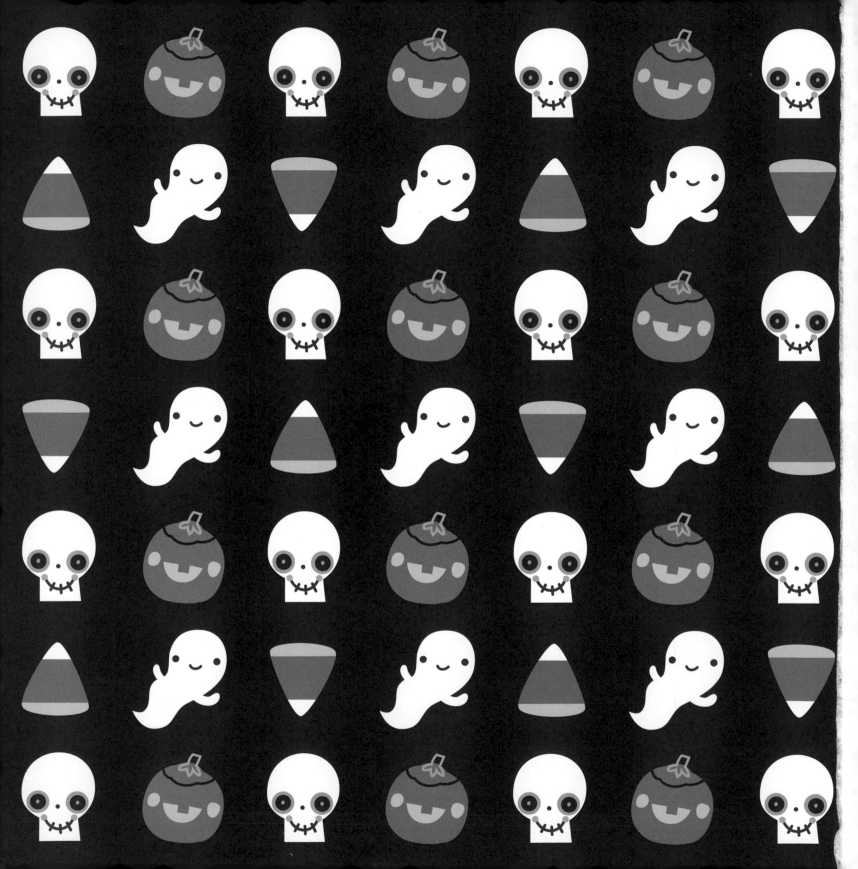

Boo! Haiku

Words by **Deanna Caswell** Pictures by **Bob Shea**

Abrams Appleseed
New York

Here's a spooky haiku just for you!

broom across the moon
pointed hat at the window
hair-raising cackle

Can you guess who from this haiku?

Boo!

It's a witch!

This witch has a spooky haiku just for you.

wings for a blanket
an upside-down nap ending
wake up! time to fly!

Can you guess who from her haiku?

Boo!
It's a bat!

This bat has a spooky haiku just for you.

a bony boogie
rattling around the room
clacking to the beat

Can you guess who from his haiku?

Boo!
It's a skeleton!

This skeleton has a spooky haiku just for you.

an orange porch pal
scooped for pie and roasted seeds
a candlelit grin

Can you guess who from his haiku?

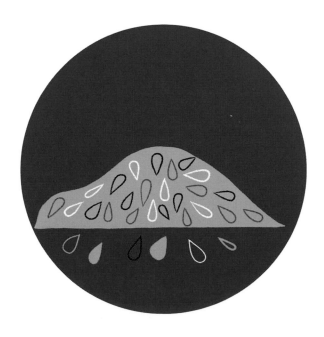

Boo!
It's a jack-o'-lantern!

This jack-o'-lantern has a spooky haiku just for you.

footsteps without feet
woo-ooo-ing in the basement
heavy chains floating

Can you guess who from his haiku?

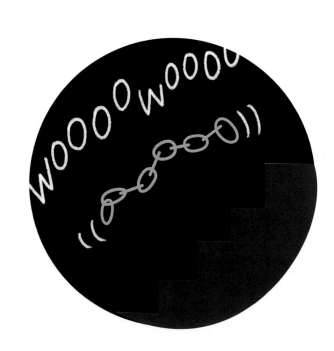

Boo!
It's a ghost!

This ghost has a spooky haiku just for you.

fence top at midnight
a whiskered shadow crossing
on soft, silent paws

Can you guess who from her haiku?

Boo!
It's a black cat!

This cat has a spooky haiku just for you.

eight legs on a web
a sticky situation
for a cornered fly

Can you guess who from his haiku?

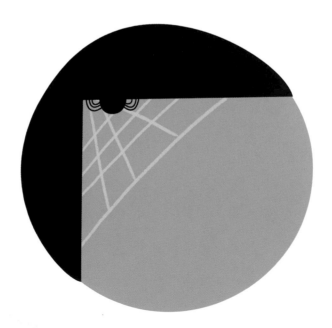

Boo!
It's a spider!

This spider has a spooky haiku just for you.

a hollowed-out tree
a feathered face in the dark
is asking *Who? Who?*

Can you guess who from her haiku?

Boo!
It's an owl!

This owl has a spooky haiku just for you.

the straw man stands guard
posted above garden rows
keeping out the birds

Can you guess who from her haiku?

Boo!
It's a scarecrow!

This scarecrow has a spooky haiku just for you.

closed door, open bags
excited painted faces
knock-knock, trick or treat!

Can you guess who from his haiku?

Boo!
It's YOU!

Haiku is a style of Japanese poetry. The *hai* in *haiku* means "to make light of" or "to make a joke of." So traditional haiku have an element of play. The haiku in this book also have a sense of play. For example, try covering the middle line of this poem and just reading the first and last lines:

a hollowed-out tree
a feathered face in the dark
is asking *Who? Who?*

Is the tree talking? If you were standing there, you wouldn't see the owl at first. He's in the dark. It would seem like the hollow in the tree was asking "Who?" Isn't that silly? Try covering the middle line of other haiku in this book!

Traditionally, haiku are three lines long. The first line has five syllables. The second line has seven syllables. The third line has five syllables again.

What's a syllable? It's a small part of a word. To find the syllables in a word, try this: Put your hand under your chin and say "hello." How many times did your chin drop? It should have dropped two times, because *hello* has two syllables: *hel-lo*. Try it with the lines of poetry in this book.

For Jack and Reid
—DC

For Ryan
—BS

Cataloging-in-Publication Data has been applied for and
may be obtained from the Library of Congress.

ISBN: 978-1-4197-2118-2

Printed and bound in China
10 9 8 7 6 5 4 3 2

For bulk discount inquiries, contact specialsales@abramsbooks.com.

ABRAMS The Art of Books
115 West 18th Street, New York, NY 10011
abramsbooks.com

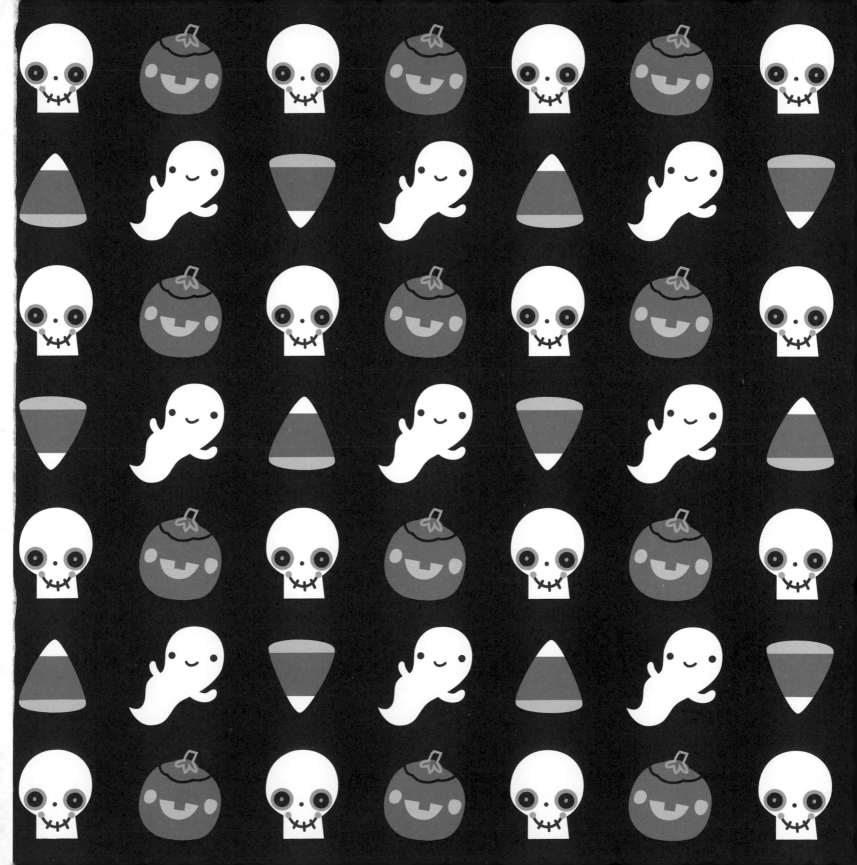

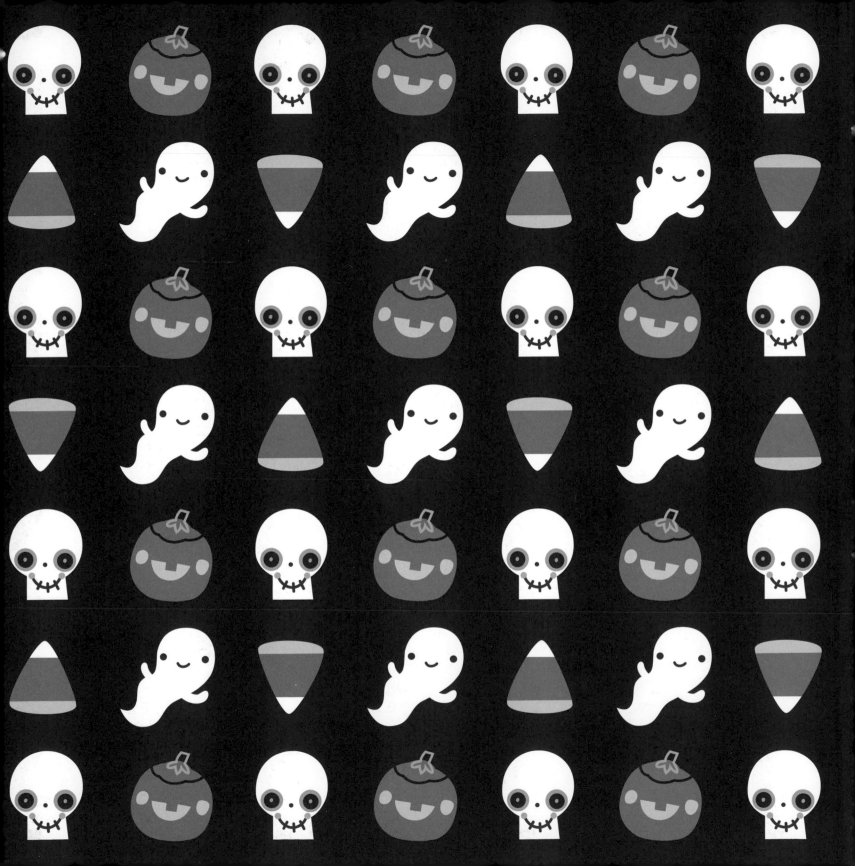